To Wonderful LOUIS

Your Aunt Casie and Uncle Josh ♡ you!

2023

THE **NORTH AMERICAN ANIMAL**

ABC
BOOK

Written & Illustrated by
MARK LUDY

Aa

Allie
the **a**lligator
absolutely **a**dores
accelerating
on her **A**TV.

Bb

Burly **B**ernie,
the **b**ig **b**uffalo,
enjoys **b**athing
in **b**ubbles.*

*We don't suggest you ever leave a buffalo unattended in a bathtub.

Cc

Carl,
the **c**offee-**c**raving
caribou, **c**uddles
with his **c**at
on the **c**ouch.

Dd

Dave,
the **d**ynamic,
doodling **d**uck,
definitely
can **d**raw!*

*Don't be discouraged if your art doesn't look like Dave's.
He's been doing this for years.

Ee

Edith the **e**el,
isn't **e**xactly **e**xcited
to wear
eyeglasses.

Ff

Frankie the **f**rog
feeds on **f**ilthy
flies, **f**illing
his **f**at **f**rame.

Gg

Gustavo,
the **g**angly
gunslingin' **g**oose,
is **g**rumpy.*

*...He's got gas.

Hh

Hank the **h**awk
happily **h**unts
on **H**ilda, **h**is **h**orse,
in **h**is **h**onkin'
huge **h**at.

Ii

Itty bitty **i**nsects,
Iggy & **I**van, are
intensely **i**nterested **in**
ice fishing.

Jj

Juniper the
jackalope
is the best
junior **j**umper
at **J**azzercise.

Kellogg,
the **k**indly
Kingfish,
is only **k**een
on **k**osher
worms.*

*I like them with ketchup.

Ll

Lu **L**u,
the **l**ollipop **l**ickin'
lizard,
lollygags in **l**ine
with her **l**uggage.

Mm

Milton,
the **m**oose
moves to his **m**usic
while **m**ulling over his
mountaineering **m**ap.

Nn

Nordy the **n**arwhal's
name is **n**otorious
as he **n**ever
takes off his
noticeable **n**ame-tag.

Oo

The **o**wls
are **o**utraged -
ornery **O**scar is still
in the **o**uthouse!

P p

Priscilla
the **p**orcupine
wants to eat her
piece of **p**izza in **p**eace,
but **P**eter the **p**ig
prattles on and on.

Qq

Queen **Q**uartilla,
the **q**uirky **q**uail,
is constantly **q**uoting
quintesential **q**uips
with her **q**uick **q**uill.

Rr

Rex the **r**attler
rests on his **r**ock
reading **r**ecipes
for **r**oasting his **r**at.

Ss

Sherman the **s**kunk
will be **s**o **s**orry
he **s**hot **S**uzy
with his
slingshot.

Tt

Turkey **T**om
tirelessly
tools about **t**own
in his **t**ow **t**ruck.

Uu

Ulysses the **U**nicorn
is **u**nderstandably **u**pset
that he is **u**nreal.*

*He's sort of sensitve about it.

Vv

Victor
the **v**ulture
is no **v**egetarian
and **v**oices
his **v**iew by **v**oting.

Ww

Wiggling in the **w**ater,
Wilbur the **w**orm
worriedly **w**onders **w**hy

...**w**hy him?

Xavier,
the **x**-tra large grizzly,
is **x**-tremely guilty
when **x**-posed
by the **x**-ray.

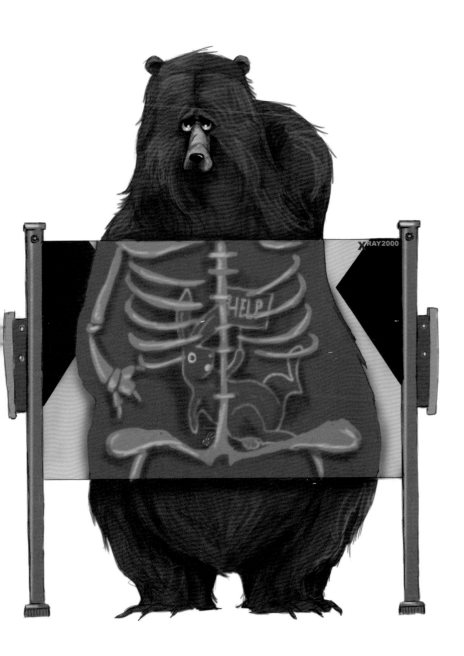

Yy

Yolanda,
the **y**ellow-jacket,
yearns to be
this **y**ear's
yo-**y**o champion.

Zz

Zeus, **Z**elda and **Z**oey
are **z**apped of energy

...time to
catch some **Z**'s.

Charlie, the **c**oyote **c**owboy, **c**uddles up to the **c**ampfire to **c**ook.

THE
END

I know... I know... It CAN'T be the END!! (Let's read it again!)